IT MAY COME AS A SHOCK

IT MAY COME AS A SHOCK

SHOCK

*Small Stories of
Moments In Life*

RONDA STEWART-MORALES

R.C. Ladybug Press, LLC

For my beloved grandmother, Lucille. I miss you.

This May Come As A Shock:
Small Stories of Moments in life
Ronda Stewart-Morales
R.C. Ladybug Press, LLC
Bronx, New York

Ronda Stewart-Morales/R.C. Ladybug Press
rc@ladybugpressllc.com
Editing by Laura Apperson
Proofreading by Sara Thwaite
Ordering Information:
Quantity sales. Special discounts are available on quantity purchases by corporations, associations, and others. For details, contact the "Special Sales Department" at the address above.
It May Come As A Shock/ Ronda Stewart-Morales —1st ed.
ISBN 978-1-0879-3843-1

INTRODUCTION

When you really look at someone in the eyes, sometimes, it is nearly impossible to know what they are struggling with on the inside. We hide behind social media, where we post smiley selfies or share an exciting update with the world, but when we close the doors and shut ourselves off from the outside world, we can suffer in silence.

There have been instances throughout my life where I was faced with challenges that left me vulnerable to daggers; both from the outside world and from my own insecurities. During my adolescence and young adult years, I was very much naive and gullible to what was in front of me, so I took everything at face value. I didn't question *why*, or strive to understand more. I simply just believed everything and everyone. I didn't know how to nourish my soul and I certainly didn't protect my heart. I didn't know it then, but I know now how much I despised myself. *Despise* may be a harsh verb to describe what I viewed, but I can recognize today how little self-love I had. That left me constantly battling; fighting the truth within me and understanding the outside world. I often think about the impact it made on me as a woman, and more important, how I overcame those obstacles with the resources that were available to me. The lessons I learned were hard, but I consider them blessings.

I wrote *It May Come as A Shock* from the perspective of what exists behind closed doors; the moments in life that many don't see, and the grapple you have with yourself to rise above. It features three short stories about how we walk around masked by happiness but deep down, we are crying for help. The collection includes different narratives that spotlight common life themes: infertility, depression, and body image.

It May Come as a Shock demonstrates the clash between societal assumption and physical and mental realization. These stories will make you consider your everyday encounters with loved ones and how compassion, empathy, and kindness can tremendously impact one's life.

It May Come as a Shock invites readers to grant themselves grace and forgiveness. This book reminds people to know that they are never alone. I created this for you, coming from me with absolute love.

CAN I?

"Negative." Not negative, again. Renee read the results of her pee-on-a-stick pregnancy test in genuine disbelief. She thought for sure that she was pregnant this time around. Frustrated, she threw the pee stick in the trash can. From the bathroom, she had a perfect view of her backyard, which was filled with butterfly bushes, hydrangeas, petunias, and imagined happiness. The early 5:30 a.m. fog and the dew settled perfectly over her manicured lawn. She took some comfort in the scenery, even though she was just hit with the unexpected devastation.

"How am I going to get through this?" she said to herself with exhaustion in her shaky voice.

She had a busy work schedule today, and it would have been easier to get through the hectic hours if she had good news on her mind. Up until recently, Renee was employed as a staff writer at the local journal. The industry was affected by the recent worldwide pandemic, and Renee was laid off as a result. Since that day, she had been freelancing as a copywriter and editor, and work had been steadily picking up. She was grateful for the back-to-back assignments on her calendar.

Renee lingered in the bathroom for a few more minutes before getting up and walking back to the bedroom feeling shame, guilt, heartache, and disappointment. Her husband Paul, who was still asleep, would still be sleeping for another hour before he headed to the nearby hospital where he worked as a registered nurse.

The past year and a half had been the hardest on Paul. Since the pandemic hit, the hospital had been overwhelmed to capacity with sick patients and devastation due to the virus. Surprisingly, Renee hadn't been worried much about Paul during this uncertain time because she knew he was meticulous and alert. Besides, safety for hospital staff was a priority, so her mind was at ease. He would tell her stories about him and his co-workers covered in personal protection equipment with every visible mucus membrane opening masked behind a cloth. Even though he sometimes worked twenty hours, he never complained.

Renee admired him so much. They had a solid relationship built on communication and gratitude. They both believed that their spirituality was the foundation of their marriage. They were true in the conviction that a higher power led their lives, and it was something to believe in strongly when they had tough days. The belief that good would always find them and acting in the space of gratitude showed up in every aspect of their lives.

Her initial plan was to surprise Paul as soon as he awoke with the positive test stick shoved in his face so it would be the first thing he saw. Instead, she went back to bed, silently whimpering to herself. There was no need to hide her pain from her husband. Renee stopped doing that years ago. Renee counted on her short fingers how long she and Paul had been enduring the torture of this pregnancy journey: seven years of testing, sonograms, surgeries, analysts, counseling, therapy, miscarriages, mentoring, research, medication, hormones, and specialists. They did anything that was required of them with full cooperation and one hundred percent effort. Renee was now forty-one. Several fertility specialists told her that she still had plenty of time, but she thought that she would have had at least two babies by now. Paul was an excellent support. He never put pressure on her to do anything she didn't want to do.

Paul was ready to walk out the door at 9:15 this morning, coffee thermos already in hand, so she decided to pretend to be busy in hopes that he wouldn't want to engage in a conversation that would give her an opportunity to cry. Renee felt the sadness built up in her throat; opening her mouth to say a word was too much and would send her over the edge. Paul simply kissed her on the top of her head, pausing for a few seconds before he walked out the door.

This morning's events were just one of many letdowns they had every twenty-eight days. Renee appreciated Paul for giving her space and time to process everything. His instincts seemed so keen and right on time. She wondered if he ever wanted to have a "normal" moment in this house—a day without mood swings, hours of crying, and depressive behavior. Paul had supported her the entire time they were trying to conceive. Even though Renee would be the one to bear their miracle, Paul took the brunt of everything else from financial burden and loss to countless late-night sessions where he talked Renee off the ledge of uncertainty. Renee for sure thought that it was the end of their relationship when they took out a second mortgage to fund one round of in-vitro fertilization in the beginning of their marriage. The procedure was unsuccessful and expensive, but Paul chocked it up to being "only money."

It was only 9:25 a.m., and she had already spent four hours of her early day consumed with baby-making thoughts. Pretty soon, her period would start, and the countdown would begin all over again. Renee closed her eyes to try to fight back the stinging tears. One minute she felt the need to say "fuck it all" and stop monitoring her ovulation days, but an inner jolt would snap her heart and head back to the reality of calculating and tracking her ovulation symptoms, like light spotting, changes in her libido, or even cervical mucus changes. Everything else in life seemed pretty seamless to Renee and Paul. They had been married for four years but had been together since she was thirty-four. They didn't have any adultery scares, health worries, or even disagreements on what to eat for dinner. They were a perfect couple on the outside, with one flawed cell on the inside. In Renee's opinion, it was her that was imperfect.

She had spent her teenage years and her twenties trying everything in her power *not* to get pregnant. Renee wasn't given the "birds and the bees" talk from her mother, but she was expected to know all there was to know about necessary precautions of premarital sex. When she was in her late teens, Renee's mother instilled the fear of her fist if she came home pregnant. That fear was a fixture in her mind every time she had sex. At that time, Renee was always on some sort of birth control. Later, in her twenties, it didn't matter that all her friends and family around her were turning up pregnant with ease. Everyone was on a different path in life, and Renee's focus was becoming a great writer. For her, it left no room for an unplanned pregnancy.

It wasn't until she met Paul that her views and focus changed. Renee got off birth control when she started dating him. He didn't object so it was unspoken that *whatever happens, happens.* Years later, the fact that nothing happened made them worry. One year into their marriage, Paul's mother flat out asked what was wrong with her. Renee felt unloved by and useless to her mother-in-law, who made it crystal clear that she wanted a grandchild from Paul. The pressure felt more and more like a strict command: *hurry up and have Paul's baby or else!* Luckily, Paul never put that same pressure on her.

Nevertheless, Renee felt like the biggest failure thinking back to the early years when she started to have concerns about her reproductive system and had to endure invasive procedures to better her changes of conceiving. First, she had a massive fibroid removed from her uterus; she had endured excruciating pain due to those fibroids and removing them would mean pain-free periods *and* a clean, ripe uterus ready to bear a child. She had scar tissue removed from her fallopian tubes. How that got there still is a mystery. Both surgeries turned out to be successful, but she had so much emotional and physical healing to do. She went through bouts of anxiety and depression during the healing process. She had time to lay on her couch, look at her swollen abdomen, and wonder if she was mentally strong enough to move forward with uncertainties and unknowns as her obstacles. After the tough and patient healing, she regained hope that she could conceive and carry to term. She couldn't help but feel defeated when it didn't happen. Renee was the only person in her family who didn't have a child. She never went to the baby showers or kids' birthday parties because it was so awkward for her. She felt like that spinster aunt that everyone pitied.

It seemed as if she had nothing in common with her close friends anymore either, since they all had kids. They were talking about bottles and breastfeeding, dance recitals, baseball practice, and the school band while she was burning the midnight oil finishing an article on a strict deadline. When she got ignorant questions about why she doesn't have any children yet, she would just respond, "Whatever is in God's plan..." It was such a bullshit excuse. The fake, forced smile she put on every day to her loved ones was such a lie.

Deep down, Renee blamed herself. She told herself that she was selfish for wanting superficial things. Renee blamed her infertility on the choices she made when she was young. No matter what her therapist told her, she *did* feel responsible. Paul had been tested for infertility three different times and his results came back normal each time. When Paul turned out to be fertile, Renee was at a loss for words. The problem was *her*. Renee didn't hide the fact that she wanted Paul to be the reason why she wasn't pregnant so her family, friends, and especially his mother would get off her case. She felt like crawling under a rock would not be good enough to hide from the shame she felt. But after a lot of testing, doctors could not pinpoint the origin of her infertility. They told her not to stress, and that it would happen. That only gave her partial relief, knowing that she didn't have any physical abnormalities, but not enough hope for a successful pregnancy.

Sometimes Renee thought that having a baby would quiet all the outside influences. She also felt the tug of war on her consciousness to have a baby for others, more than for herself. That, too, would satisfy the scarring of feeling like a freak. When she was alone, she would sometimes question why she spent every waking moment trying to get pregnant; was it something that she really wanted? If she could not conceive, would her life be enough?

A few weeks later, Renee was sitting at her kitchen table with her herbal tea, just staring at the wall. She wondered if she should take a break from trying to conceive. Maybe it was time put away the charts, thermometers, and apps and just...*be*. Today, she was ovulating and she was tired and exasperated. Paul was due home soon and knowing that he had had a long day already, she didn't want to pounce on him before he had the chance to eat dinner.

"Why don't we take a break, babe?" Renee had asked Paul earlier that morning.

"Do you *want* to take a break?" Paul had responded, looking into her eyes.

"I don't really know. Frankly, I'm kinda over the whole process," Renee had answered while rubbing her eyes.

"Whatever you want to do, babe. I'm good with whatever," Paul whispered. "I gotta go, see you tonight." He then kissed her on her forehead and left.

While Renee sat at her table, she thought about the times when she was younger and carefree with her sexual escapades. She gave a weak smile to herself as she reflected on the moments when she felt happy, not bothered with outside distractions, like all the people who felt it was appropriate to express to her what was best for her. At that very moment, Renee got a jolt of warmth through her body, an indicator that she was still young and anything was possible for her family. She vowed to reincorporate love and happiness in her and Paul's lovemaking. More important, she wanted to incorporate love into their home! Renee had an instant understanding of what she needed to do for herself: take this journey, and life in general, day by day.

Renee let out a long exhale after her epiphany. No wonder Paul was so cool and collected; he had chosen to not overwhelm himself with the what-ifs. With or without a baby, they were going to be just fine. Renee felt it. When Paul arrived home, Renee hugged him tight. It signified that her mind, body, and soul were at ease. Renee could feel the relief in Paul as he embraced her back. Today, it was about *them*.

A week and a half or so later, in the early morning, Renee found herself standing in her bathroom again. Again, she sat on the toilet. This time when she glanced out the window, it was pitch black, and she was unable to see the colorful blooms that she knew were there. She just wanted to look at something different. To remind herself that what she was feeling was real. She didn't wipe the tears that streamed down her cheeks and past her neck. She took a deep breath and stood up, knowing she had been there long enough. She gripped the pee stick tight with one hand and held onto the sink with the other. Renee stared at herself in the mirror and tried to compose her face before walking out and facing Paul. She has done this a hundred times; why would today be any different? Without thinking, Renee looked down at the pee stick then placed it on the counter. She could've thrown it away, but her mind was not reasoning. She quickly closed her eyes to give herself a moment. She told herself that whatever the result was, she was accepting. Her heart was pounding what seemed to be a thousand beats per second. To gain control, she again took a deep breath and opened her eyes. *Positive.* Renee wiped her face with her bare hand and turned the knob to walk out of the bathroom.

MONDAY AFTERNOON

Mickey was already late for work, and he had forgotten to make sure he had enough credit on his metro card. He dug so deep into his coat pockets to find loose change that he only came up with a wad of lint. He checked the inside of his breast pocket, hoping he would hit the jackpot. *Nothing.*

Mickey pulled out his cellphone to check the time: 8:14 a.m. His face hardened with disappointment when he realized how late it was. Mickey had at least a thirty-minute ride to the other side of the city to the grocery store where he stocked shelves. His shift started at 8:30 a.m. After seven years riding the same train to his crummy job, this had never happened to him before.

Mickey could hear the train approaching the track, and he had to be on it. He decided to take the chance and run through the emergency gate without paying. He ran up the stairs to the train platform, hoping there weren't any undercover cops watching the entrance. Mickey was visibly overweight and out of shape, so much so that he almost keeled over at the top of the stairs. Before he had an opportunity to sit on the available bench, he saw a train approaching the platform. Mickey let out a heavy sigh of relief. Even though it was no more than thirty degrees outside, Mickey felt a quick rush of heat spread through his chest. Completely exhausted and out of breath, Mickey held himself up by holding onto the platform wall for support and gently wiped the thin film of sweat from his forehead.

Mickey just shook his head in disbelief, with no effort whatsoever to move mountains. He didn't even bother to calculate the new estimated arrival time to the grocery store since he was already late. Once the train arrived and he found an empty seat, he took out his headphones and plugged them into the cellphone jack. "That's the Way of the World" by Earth, Wind & Fire roared through his earbuds, and it could not have come at a more appropriate moment. He allowed the lyrics to penetrate his mind as he closed his eyes tight to listen carefully:

...Looking back, we've touched on sorrowful days

Future pass, they disappear...

Tears filled Mickey's eyes, and it was too late to hold them back. He quickly wiped them away with his sleeve cuff. The song reminded him of his share of struggles and obstacles throughout his life, starting with his unconventional and unlucky childhood. Both his parents were addicted to heroin and contracted the AIDS virus. He was only nine years old when he became an orphan. That's an age where you need so much guidance, direction, support, and, most important, love.

Mickey had never experienced family support, which most folks take for granted. He didn't have any extended family besides his maternal grandmother and he was his parents' only child. Even though he felt the job at the grocery store was grueling, having a friend in his manager, Mr. Sanchez, was the most joy he felt in his life. He leaned back, closed his eyes, and reminisced on the first time he met Mr. Sanchez.

Mickey was a customer at his store. He was shopping for a few things and noticed a "now hiring" sign in the window. Mickey was desperately looking for work and didn't much care what the job entailed. He approached someone who appeared to be a worker to inquire about the opening.

"Excuse me, who do I speak with regarding the sign you have in the window?" Mickey asked. The guy he asked was short, stubby, overweight, and had deep, narrowing dark eyes. He had stubble on his face and smelled of cooking grease. He sized Mickey up and down with an unnecessary scowl.

"You can talk to me," the worker answered bluntly.

"My name is Mickey," Mickey said with a slight smile while extending his hand. The guy snickered through his teeth while rolling his eyes.

"Fill out this application," the guy said, shoving a blank application to Mickey without accepting the handshake.

Mickey took the application and walked towards the door. He didn't want trouble or to start an argument with someone he would potentially be working with. He had already decided he would fill the application out at home and bring it back. As he was walking out, he was stopped by another worker. This one seemed more put together and less scruffy.

"Hey there, son, my name is Carlos Sanchez. I see you have an application," Mr. Sanchez said, pointing to the paper.

"Right," Mickey managed to say. "I was just gonna fill this out and bring it back."

From the corner of Mickey's eye, he saw the man who gave him the application staring at him intensely.

Who is this asshole?! Mickey screamed in his head.

"That's not necessary; you can fill it out right here and I'll take it from you," Mr. Sanchez said as he led him to the back of the store.

"I am the owner, by the way," Mr. Sanchez said matter-of-factly.

"I'm Mickey," he said quickly.

Mr. Sanchez led Mickey through the double doors to the back office. The office had a desktop computer monitor with smaller monitors around it. Immediately Mickey recognized the smaller monitors to be security for the whole store. A couple monitors were facing the cash registers up front, one faced the safe in the back office, a couple faced the front door, and two faced the back stocking area. One particular camera was facing a worktable that was also in the back room. Mickey found it odd that a camera was placed to watch the worktable. Mr. Sanchez noticed Mickey looking at his monitors and Mickey quickly turned away and sat at the table.

"Why don't you fill this out and tell me a little about yourself?" Mr. Sanchez instructed.

"There isn't much to tell, really," Mickey said without taking his eyes off of his paper. The truth was, Mickey was embarrassed. He didn't have the best childhood and adulthood wasn't looking much better. Mickey figured that he would give Mr. Sanchez some background since he seemed so nice and was giving him the opportunity to apply for this job.

Mickey sensed a calmness in Mr. Sanchez; his genuine interest in getting to know him. It was comforting to Mickey. He felt like Mr. Sanchez was someone he could trust. Someone who seemed to pass no judgment on him. He hopefully could call Mr. Sanchez a true friend as well as an employer. Before he knew it, Mickey told him about his past, and he hoped that the gloomy details wouldn't affect his potential employment. Mickey explained that he was orphaned when he was only nine years old, then sent to live with his grandmother. The both of them lived in a one-bedroom unit in the projects. She did the bare minimum for Mickey: food, clothes, shelter. All business, no love. For many years, Mickey felt his grandmother resented him and his presence; believing his existence somehow had something to do with his mother's downfall and decline. It was all speculation, nothing was confirmed for sure, and he never asked her.

Mickey told Mr. Sanchez that he had a five-year-old daughter that he didn't have much of a relationship with. He wasn't sure if he should be too candid with Mr. Sanchez about all his issues but he felt an over-whelming sense of comfort. Even if he didn't get the job, it felt good to share his life with someone who wanted to listen. He went on to share that the child support bureau threatened him that he would need to obtain trackable employment if he wanted to stay out of jail for not paying child support for his daughter. His only option was to get a square gig.

Mr. Sanchez listened intensely with no interruptions and with warmth in his eyes. Mickey assumed Mr. Sanchez's heart was softened when he learned about Mickey's dilemma. When Mickey was finished, he let out a sigh of relief, and the room fell deadly silent. Mr. Sanchez didn't ask any questions nor did he break eye contact. He simply patted Mickey on the shoulder and smiled.

"Thanks for sharing, Mic. May I call you Mic? Let me know when you are finished with the application," Mr. Sanchez finally said as he rose from his chair and walked away without even waiting for a response. Mickey was left with some dignity and appreciated Mr. Sanchez for showing him respect. After Mickey finished his application, Mr. Sanchez hired him that day. He gave Mickey the rundown of the place, told him that he would be stocking, and introduced him to the other employees, including the cranky man Mickey had met when he first approached the store.

"Mickey, this is Will. He is my assistant manager here. You take your directives from him," Mr. Sanchez explained. Will just stood there as if he wanted more of an introduction. He had the same disgusting scowl on his face as when Mickey first met him. Mickey could immediately tell that this Will character was not impressed nor was he thrilled that Mickey was there.

"You can call me Mic," he said, as he tried to shake his hand again. Mickey liked the fact that Mr. Sanchez gave him a nickname; he felt like he had some sort of a brotherhood with someone for the first time in his life and he wanted to spread that over through Will with hopes to smooth the awkwardness.

"When can you start...Mickey?" Will said with a slight pause. Again, he had no interest in shaking Mickey's hand.

"I can start immediately," Mickey said enthusiastically.

"Be here at 8:30 a.m. sharp tomorrow," Will said and threw two clean aprons at him.

Mickey looked at Mr. Sanchez for some sort of intervention or explanation of why his assistant manager was being such a dick. But Mr. Sanchez just shrugged his shoulders.

"*Asshole,*" Mickey murmured as he and Mr. Sanchez walked away.

Back in the present day, on the train on his way to work, Mickey shook his head to himself as he remembered his first meeting with Will. Seven years later, the relationship between them was still the same, maybe a little worse. Will and Mickey never shared personal stories with each other. They never went to lunch together and Will didn't exhibit a mentor/mentee relationship with Mickey. Even after all that time, they really didn't know much about one another.

Mickey had been working there six days a week for the last seven years and made enough to rent a small room from a couple of people he knew from his neighborhood. He had been rotating the same two pairs of jeans and three T-shirts for the past seven years. He had the same pair of sneakers for the last four years and stolen the coat he was currently wearing from a terminated employee who left it in their locker at the grocery store. Mr. Sanchez gifted Mickey the cell phone he was using, an iPhone 5 that still was in decent shape. He knew Mr. Sanchez wouldn't be at the door to ream his ass about being so late. It was Monday morning, the busiest time of the day and week. He hoped even Will would be too busy to lecture Mickey on being late. Mondays had the most vendor deliveries, the most customer traffic, the most cash transactions. It was so busy that Mr. Sanchez had to be at the store at 5:30 a.m. to sign invoices, and he wanted all hands on deck on Mondays.

Mickey didn't have a set position at the store. He did it all: janitor, bagger, delivery guy, stocker, price checker, spill cleaner, deli clerk, window washer, and anything else Mr. Sanchez wanted him to do.

Mr. Sanchez was a sixty-seven-year-old widow who probably was all of five feet tall and one hundred and thirty pounds soaking wet. He was feisty and fierce but fair. He ran a tight ship at the store and didn't tolerate bullshit. He didn't trust anyone else to check the vendor deliveries, not even his store managers—including Will. A few years back, Will mishandled a couple of the register trays and some cash was not accounted for. Since then, Will wasn't allowed to handle the money. After the incident, Mr. Sanchez did not accuse Will of being dishonest, but he chastised him in the back in front of several employees, including Mickey, for not being more careful and professional. Will didn't appreciate it at all. Will's animosity and jealousy toward Mickey inflamed after that incident. It was obvious that Mickey and Mr. Sanchez were close, and Will would do anything to prove to Mr. Sanchez that

Mickey was trash and he himself was the prince of the store. Mickey was hip to Will's game and wasn't at all concerned. He and Mr. Sanchez were for sure close, but Mr. Sanchez never played favorites and simply appreciated Mickey's hard work and dedication.

When Mickey arrived at the store, he decided to go in through the service door in the back. He knew that there would be a lot of traffic with deliveries so he figured he would slip in without being noticed. Mickey made it to the lockers but saw Will standing at the worktable peeling back pieces of an apple with a dirty box cutter. Mickey turned back to the locker with his eyes shut tight while he shoved his coat inside. Before he closed the locker, he knew Will was approaching him because he could smell the familiar scent of old grease. Will pressed his back against the lockers and turned to Mickey with a smirk.

"You are late, Mic," Will said with a mouthful of apple, some of which landed on Mickey's shirt as he talked.

"It's *Mickey*. I'm sorry, the train was late, and..." Mickey replied. Mickey felt that Will didn't have permission to call him "Mic" ever since their first encounter years ago. Will knew that calling him by his now-popular nickname would boil Mickey's blood. Without finishing his explanation, Will interrupted him by waving the box cutter in Mickey's face.

"I don't give a shit. If you want to work here, you betta be on time. Otherwise, I will have to let you go and Mr. Sanchez won't be able to save you," Will said with venom in his voice.

Will tossed the half-eaten apple in the trash can but missed. He walked away without even picking it up. Mickey kept his eyes glued on Will as he tossed the box cutter on the worktable before disappearing through the double doors. "Fucking asshole," Mickey said out loud.

Mickey took the apron out from the locker, hung his head, and put it around his broad body. Mickey didn't need instructions on what to do on a day-to-day basis. There were dozens of boxes that needed to be opened and stocked on the shelf. Mickey was already behind and knew that he would spend most of the day and evening stocking and cleaning up the aftermath. He anticipated being at the store until at least midnight. The thought of the fourteen-hour day almost made him cry. At minimum wage plus overtime, he would still see a mediocre check next week; he would have just enough left over for a six-pack of Miller Lite.

Blood started to rise to his head, and he felt his face sting in heat as he thought about his finances. He slammed the locker door in frustration. In addition to his run-in with Will and his prediction on the long day ahead, he was already in a bad mood. Mickey felt the world collapsing around him. No family, no sustainable relationship with a woman, no place of his own, and no real money saved. He couldn't rely on Mr. Sanchez to clean up his life, especially since he had been so generous already.

Alcohol for sure was Mickey's unconditional friend. Gin, vodka, rum, tequila, it didn't matter. They kept him company after work and when he wasn't scheduled to work at all. He was getting bored with nightly intoxication, but at this point, it was a necessity to stay lit because the intense morning body shakes and violent vomiting of bile were getting too much to handle. Sometimes, a half-cup of cheap bourbon in his morning coffee kept him even and fortunately got him through the days working at the store with Will's micromanaging. He had to be careful because if Mr. Sanchez found out that he periodically drank before work, he would be out on his ass and have no one to blame but himself. Mickey felt that he led the life of a fifty-year-old alcoholic with a life expectancy of another two years. His face was sunken, his belly was bloated, the whites of his eyes were brown, and his teeth were falling out.

Mickey scanned the boxes lined up against the concrete wall. It looked like it was just him today working in the back. Usually, there were two other stockers on Monday to help, but maybe there were call-outs. Will was probably in the front of the house, so he was grateful to have this time in the back by himself. Mickey started opening the boxes to the left and worked his way down the line. *Cut box, load dolly, stock shelf, repeat.*

After being soaked in sweat from marathon stocking, Mickey

decided to take a five-minute breather. He looked at the digital clock on the work desk, and it read 2:03 p.m. What he wanted was a shot of tequila to set him up until the evening. Mickey knew that it wouldn't happen anytime soon.

He was feeling terrible lately—his stomach churned from hunger, or perhaps it was from the alcohol abuse and drinking cheap beer. His teeth seemed to be in rough shape; cavities and decay, headaches and tightness in his chest. He wouldn't be surprised if he suffered from high blood pressure. He really needed to make an appointment to see a physician. He had to shake the fear he had over the doctor telling him how many diseases he had in his body. Mickey went to the small fridge that was under the worktable to see if anyone left food for him to take and eat. When he bent down to open the refrigerator door, he accidentally knocked over some items onto the floor from the worktable, including a calculator, a sharpie, and the box cutter. He picked up everything and placed them back on the table.

Mickey stared long at the box cutter. There were still small shards of apple on the sharp blade. God only knows what other uses Will had for it. Mickey rolled his eyes at the thought of the despicable things Will possibly did with the cutter. Mickey ran his calloused thumb on the ridge to extract and close the blade. Then he moved faster to open it. *Slower. Faster.* Mickey stared blankly at the wall in that moment of silence he had. He took his thoughts back to his tough childhood with his grandmother, where he was treated like a second-class relative in a home where he was supposed to be protected. Then he had flashes of his memories with Mr. Sanchez. Mickey remembered the times that he and Mr. Sanchez laughed at their inside jokes, how they worked side by side on large store projects, and how they sometimes shared lunch and talked about everything or nothing at all. Mickey smiled, but the smile was quickly replaced with a sullen frown. He wished for something bigger and better for his life. He couldn't hide behind Mr. Sanchez for the rest of his life, and Will was no sooner becoming his ally. A rush of warmth rushed through Mickey's body and on impulse, Mickey held the cutter in his left hand with the blade exposed and moved it toward his right arm. He could feel his legs wobble and buckle. They felt like Jell-O under his waist. Hot tears ran down his cheeks, and he did nothing to stop them. He leaned over the table for balance, closed his eyes tight, and bit his bottom lip.

There's someone back here! Mickey said to himself. Suddenly, there was the sound of fast, shuffling feet from the direction of Mr. Sanchez's office. Mickey felt a jolt of humiliation when he realized that he was never alone. Mr. Sanchez must have seen him the whole time on the security monitor. He quickly closed the blade and used his filthy apron to wipe his wet face.

"Are you almost done in the frozen section? I have an end cap I want you to stock with tuna cans that just came in. They are on sale this week," Mr. Sanchez said with a shaky voice as he approached the worktable. He was as white as a ghost and his eyes were wide.

"Yeah, I'm done. I'm going to bring them out," Mickey said in a quiet voice. His hand was still on the blade, but he moved it away when he realized Mr. Sanchez was closer to him than he thought.

"I'll help you, Mic," Mr. Sanchez replied as he guided him from the table with his hand on his back. "I'll help you," Mr. Sanchez repeated. This time he had Mickey in a semi-embrace.

Mickey allowed Mr. Sanchez to escort him to the front of the store. He would gladly accept his assistance.

MONSTER

I've never liked my body, and I especially hate how I look in jeans. My legs are too short, my thighs are too big, and my waist and butt are not proportionate. I remember the times I actually went to the store to shop for clothes. Those days are long gone now. I usually waited until I had barely any decent jeans left, with wear and tear in the crotch and thigh area starting to appear, before I dragged my ass to the store to look for another pair. So when that finally happened, there I was in the Aeropostale dressing room at the mall, crying on the outside, ready to fall apart on the inside. The four-way mirrors in the dressing rooms reminded me of the circus mirrors that create optical illusions when you stand in front of them. I stood on the carpeted pedestal, surrounded by the reflection of my flaws staring back at me. I turned to the left to get a glimpse, and I cringed. I sucked my stomach in a little and turned to my right, and grimaced. Oh, how I dreaded going jean shopping! See, this is the number one reason why I shop online. In the privacy of my own home, I have the ability to tear myself to shreds without having to hide my tears and frustration.

In my eyes, I am the poster child of awkward. My mom always said that I would "thin out" because I was a young twenty-nine-year-old, and my body had to "grow into itself," whatever that meant. She was trying to be polite. My mom always is cautious when talking to me about body image. She is honest but respectful, and I was grateful for her selective words. I tried to appreciate my God-given curves, but I always thought there could be fine-tuning in some areas. For example, I hadn't had any children yet, so I didn't understand why I was battling a full pouch in my lower abdomen area. The dimples on the sides of my hips are at the first stages of cellulite, and my inner thighs rub, not just touch. I could go on and on about the hideous grooves and dents that somehow only I can see.

My little sister always asked me to go with her to the mall to get new clothes, and I always respectfully declined her offers. Who finds that shit enjoyable?! Even though she was two years younger than me, she was already as tall as I was. I longed for her physique: perfect rounded breasts, a slim waist that she doesn't have to try hard to maintain, and evenly proportioned hips. Many thought that she isn't naturally blessed with her body, but she is the real deal. She is not self-conscious at all. She doesn't worry about her body or weight and seems confident in everything she wears. I don't even think she cares that she is envied. My sister is humble and considerate and is conscientious about what she says around me. Somehow she figured out how much I loathe my body, and she silently takes my feelings into consideration. Ugh, I love her so much. I don't understand how we grew up in the same household and developed opposite body images.

I believe that everything in my life is a result of my thoughts, feelings, and actions. I spent countless days and nights for most of my adolescent years wishing I had a different figure. Looking through images on social media and watching reality shows where no one seems to be "natural" took a serious toll on my psyche. In my early teens, I told myself that it was not real, that I can't believe everything I see and watch. But over time, the more I engaged, the more I wanted to match what I saw. My mom would say all the time, "Baby, do you know how long it takes for those girls to look like that? How many pictures it took to get the *right* one? How many filters, enhancements, and alterations it took to make themselves *perfect*? No one in this world is born that flawless, baby."

I thought I knew how far to go with my harmful ideologies. I never binged and purged or starved myself; however, I still had lingering repugnant thoughts in my mind about doing something drastic to myself. I admit that I created this. I imagined having a body that wasn't achievable for me. When I reached my twenties, I filled out for the most part as my mom predicted, but I wanted to be "perfect." I constantly had to replay my mother's words in my head to keep from going too far, but some other force took over most of the time.

I dated men who would feed my subconscious with desires that I couldn't quite manifest. I brought that insanity into my heart. I remember being a young twenty-one-year-old, and my boyfriend at the time would watch all the hip-hop videos and compare the video vixens to me. Every time he would mention how long a model's hair was or how sexy another girl was or how big and beautiful a girl's butt was, I sank deeper and deeper into self-esteem destruction. It didn't take long for my subconscious to meet with my conscious, and I truly believed and wanted to look like someone else. "Why would anyone do something so horrible?" many would say. My theory was he was not mature enough to see the damage he was causing.

The spiral started; I was adamant about changing my appearance, but when I first had those thoughts, I didn't know how I wanted to change. I didn't have a foundation, a muse, guidance: all components of knowing *exactly* what you want in life. All I knew was I wanted something different. I was walking on a tightrope of creating and potentially damaging myself emotionally, spiritually, as well as physically. I was definitely not in control of my emotions nor did I have the patience to know what I needed to love myself.

I developed an obsession with perfection. I constantly people-watched, looking at other women that passed me. I looked at their hair, nails, lips, tits, ass, legs, and everything in between. I compared random strangers' thighs to my thighs. I picked apart my body and looked at others, wondering if they had something about their bodies they would like to change. I wanted to change everything. I wanted to eliminate the circus mirroring that I saw every day when I stared at my reflection.

My mom and sister said therapy would help. Telling me I would learn mechanisms on how not to be so self-destructive. Explaining that over time and with tolerance, I would learn to appreciate myself for who I was and what I looked like. Deep down, I knew they were right. But since I'd spent countless years trying to reach a level that took so much effort to achieve, I didn't want anyone to change my mind. It was too late to convince me otherwise.

I expressed my concerns to plastic surgeon Dr. Sheer last month. I gave him pictures cut out from magazines of what I wanted my new body to resemble. I had heard about Dr. Sheer from a social media post. His before and after pictures were astounding, and I wanted to be the next example. Dr. Sheer indulged me. We worked together to develop what I wanted to see when I woke up. His consultation, encouragement, and expertise were all the therapy I needed. Dr. Sheer had to be only a few years older than I was; he was striking in the face and had a fit physique. Us being around the same age, I felt he could relate to me. I told Dr. Sheer everything I wanted done: double chin removal; breast implants and lift; liposuction in arms, abdomen, hips, thighs, and back; abdominal and waist sculpting and tightening; and a butt lift. The fantastic thing about plastic surgeons is they never pass judgment and try to talk you out of your decision. Maybe because they don't have any personal investment in their patients, and it's their business to generate as much revenue as possible. Talking me out of my procedures would be money out of his pocket.

Nevertheless, Dr. Sheer tried to make me feel at ease. He saw the pain in my eyes and listened when I poured out the hatred I had for my body. That was the most expensive therapy session I ever had. I drained my bank account but, it will be worth it, I thought. I wanted to remind myself why I am going through this procedure. First, I had to tell myself that the ugly duckling who hated to try on jeans was a beautiful person. Then, I had to speak the words aloud. With that solidification, I could now move on to the next chapter. Dr. Sheer would for sure catapult me there. My mother and sister surprisingly were very supportive of my decision. I came to the conclusion that they would rather have me with my phony sense of satisfaction than not have me around at all.

My father doesn't want to know anything about it. He doesn't understand my reasoning and tells me I am beautiful the way I look. But, of course, he would say that! He's my father, and he is obligated to say nothing less. My parents are still together, and it is impressive that after thirty years of marriage, my dad still looks at my mom as if she were a chiseled goddess. I would watch her at the sink washing dishes, and he would sneak up behind her, move in close, wrap his hands around her waist, and admire her natural beauty. Mom is grateful that Dad still finds her attractive but, deep down, wishes she had fewer fine wrinkles and visible stretch marks. I want *that*! I want the self-esteem that my mother possessed.

"Baby, you have to appreciate God's masterpiece. You are the most beautiful girl," my mother would say to me all the time. She never missed a moment to remind me of who I really was and not who I thought I should be.

I wanted to believe her. I *desperately* wanted to have her words ring true in my heart, but the poison I fed myself for so many years had a strong hold on me. I told her that I would try to do better, but we both knew that I didn't try hard enough. So, this quick fix was my only solution.

"I hope you did your research, baby girl! You have to make sure that these doctors have the expertise and skills to perform the procedures. Not every doctor is the right doctor," my mother warned.

I did go so far as to make sure Dr. Sheer was board-certified, state-approved, critically acclaimed, and whatever else these physicians are these days. Pictures speak a thousand words, and those women didn't mention any complications.

"This is common nowadays, Mom. No need to worry," I said to Mom in the most calming voice as I could. I wanted her to be at ease and I wanted me to be happy.

After Dr. Sheer made his markings all over my body pre-op, I took a glance in the small mirror above his shoulder to see. I resembled the Joker or even the Marvel villain Thanos with the markings on my face, neck, chest, midsection, and lower body. I frowned, then cried. Dr. Sheer asked me if I was still willing to go through with the procedure, and I told him that I was okay. I was crying for so many reasons. I cried for the memories of me bunkering in my house for weeks on end during the summers to avoid wearing bathing suits and less clothing. I cried when men told me that I would look better if I went to the gym. I cried because I was going to be given a brand-new face and look. Someone that I wouldn't recognize or know. I cried because I would have to introduce my inner self to my new outer self and was terrified if both would get along or not. Would I accept the new face staring back at me in the mirror? The truth was that I wasn't afraid of what others saw me as, I was afraid of myself, of what would emerge after the doctor cut and stitched. Somehow the ugliness I saw would merge with the innocence I ignored and as a result, I would ironically morph into something unrecognizable. Would I be able to live the rest of my life with this new creation from a stranger?

A sense of uncontrollable anxiety hit me straight in the chest. *Was this a good idea*? I blotted my tears, ensuring I didn't make the blue marker run on my face, messing up Dr. Sheer's guidelines. I wasn't concerned about Dr. Sheer's capabilities. Instead, I was worried that my security wouldn't improve. I was terrified that my soul would instantly reject what I was not and continue this vicious cycle of perfectionism. Hopefully, I would have to do this only once. I was young, and my body would adjust.

I don't remember the nurses leading me into the operation room. I don't remember laying on the gurney, and I can't recall having the IV needle inserted into my arm. I'm foggy about the oxygen mask being placed over my nose and mouth. I do not remember waking up from the medically induced sleep. There were complications from the surgery, and I lost a lot of blood. I also developed an infection in my abdomen that spread to all my organs. My body was not strong enough to withstand the hours of anesthesia plus the trauma it endured.

I want to see what I will look like; I am eager to take the bandages off and see a different canvas beyond the visible bruising. I yearn to run my fingers over my smoothed, stretched skin. I wonder if my parents and sister are proud to see what I look like despite my insecurities and reservations about doing the surgery. My mother, for sure, will be happy with the results. My sister will be jealous. God, I just want to see how I will look in jeans.

ABOUT THE AUTHOR

Ronda Stewart-Morales was born in Buffalo, New York. She began writing in high school and grew as a freelance writer, joining contributing networks such as *Yahoo!* She lives in the New York City with area with her husband and I*t May Come As A Shock* is her first collection of short stories.